For Sammy, with love – L.R.

To Alex and Dave – G.G.

Picture Kelpies is an imprint of Floris Books. First published in 2013 by Floris Books.
Text © Lynne Rickards. Illustrations © Gabby Grant. Lynne Rickards and Gabby Grant assert their right
under the Copyright, Designs and Patent Act 1988 to be identified as the Author and Illustrator of this Work.
All rights reserved. No part of this publication may be reproduced without the prior permission of
Floris Books, 15 Harrison Gardens, Edinburgh www.florisbooks.co.uk
The publisher acknowledges subsidy from Creative Scotland towards the publication of this volume.
British Library CIP Data available. ISBN 978-086315-952-7. Printed in China

Harris the Hero

Lynne Rickards
and Gabby Grant

Picture Kelpies

Harris the puffin loved living at sea.
There really was no place that he'd rather be.

But ever since Lewis, his brother, left home,
poor Harris was feeling quite sad and alone.

Everyone else seemed so happily paired,
while Harris thought sadly that nobody cared.

One day he decided
he'd take a quick trip:
perhaps he'd go fishing,
or follow a ship.

He might hitch a ride on a hot-air balloon,
or hop on a rocket and fly to the moon...

He wanted adventure!
He wanted some fun!
But mostly he missed
being close to someone.

He took to the air and it carried him high.
Like most other seabirds, he just loved to fly!

He dodged a wild golf ball at Balcomie Green,
then sailed over Crail on a breeze that was keen.

The sight of bright sailboats was one he liked best.
In Anstruther harbour he stopped for a rest.

Anstruther

Balcomie Links

Crail

Isle of May

N

"Help!" called a timid voice somewhere nearby,
"Please help me, I'm lost," and it started to cry.

Harris soon spotted a pair of dark eyes
on a sweet baby seal of the tinicst size!

"I drifted too far, so I'm glad to see you!
My mum will be missing me –
what should I do?"

"Where do you live, little seal?" Harris said.
"I live on an island with one rocky head.

But now I can't find it. Which way should I go?"
Well, Harris looked round, and then answered, "I know!

It must be that island out east I can see.
Don't worry," he smiled, "you can just follow me."

So Harris set off, flying slowly and low,
to show the young seal where he needed to go.

The water got choppy –
the waves were immense!
Poor Harris had fears
that his plan made no sense.

The baby seal struggled,
now quite out of puff.
"I'm not sure I'll make it –
I'm not strong enough."

Just then, Harris spotted a short piece of wood.
He flew down and pulled it as hard as he could.

"Hold this, little seal – it will keep you from sinking."
"Well done!" said a voice, "That was very quick thinking!"

And up splashed a fish with a bit of seaweed:
"Tie this to the wood and we'll pull for more speed."

While Harris flew on, gripping hard with his beak,
the fish sped below like a quick silver streak.

They pulled and they pulled, and the seal held on tight.
Both fish and bird struggled with all of their might!

Then a dolphin popped up and said, "Here's how it's done!
We dolphins know how to make rescuing fun!"

The next thing to land was
a big eider duck,
and the seal pup could hardly
believe his good luck!

Two otters arrived at the very same time:
"Relax, little seal – you are going to be fine!"

They all crowded round him and swept him along.
When the team worked as one,
they were speedy and strong!

In minutes, the seal's island came into view.
A thankful voice called, "We've been looking for you!"

The baby seal flopped on a rock to recover,
and got a big welcoming hug from his mother!

The dolphin and otters, the duck and the fish
were proud to have helped the young seal with his wish.

The team had succeeded! Their mission was done,
and Harris said, "Thanks for your help, everyone!"

By now he was pretty exhausted as well.
He thought he might stay where he was for a spell.

This place was like none he'd encountered before,
with guillemots, razorbills, puffins galore!

"You're such a kind puffin," a gentle voice said.
When Harris turned round, her white face went quite red!

"You think so?" asked Harris.
"That's lovely to hear.

But really, I'm not
all that special, I fear."

"You ARE!" cried the seals,
"You have saved one of us!
And like it or not,
we are making a fuss!"

"Come see the whole island – I'll show you around,"
said Isla, the puffin friend Harris had found.

They soared through the air over sparkling seas,
steep cliffs and green grasses that waved in the breeze.

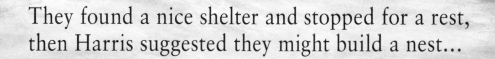

They found a nice shelter and stopped for a rest,
then Harris suggested they might build a nest...

From Isla's pink cheeks, he was able to guess
that her answer to that was a definite YES!

Well, Harris was happy to start a new life,
with lots of good friends and a wonderful wife.

It just goes to show
that whatever you do,
if you help someone else,
it might just help you too!